BORIS
GETS A LIZARD

by Andrew Joyner

SCHOLASTIC INC.

ADVENTURES ARE ALWAYS JUST AROUND THE CORNER WITH *BORIS*!

Table of Contents

No part of this publication may be reproduced, stored in a retrieval system, or transmitted in any form or by any means, electronic, mechanical, photocopying, recording, or otherwise, without written permission of the publisher. For information regarding permission, write to Puffin Books, a division of Penguin Group (Australia), 250 Camberwell Road, Camberwell, Victoria 3124, Australia.

Library of Congress Cataloging-in-Publication Data

Joyner, Andrew.
Boris gets a lizard / Andrew Joyner.
p. cm. – (Boris ; 2)
Originally published: Camberwell, Victoria, Australia : Puffin, c2011.
Summary: Boris has a lot of pets, but what he really wants is a Komodo dragon, so he comes up with a plan—and invites his class to come and see his lizard.
ISBN 978-0-545-48447-3 — ISBN 978-0-545-48446-6
1. Warthog–Juvenile fiction. 2. Komodo dragon–Juvenile fiction. 3. Lizards–Juvenile fiction.
[1. Warthog–Fiction. 2. Komodo dragon–Fiction. 3. Lizards–Fiction.] I. Title.
PZ7.J8573Bop 2013
823.92–dc23
2012034232

ISBN 978-0-545-48446-6 (hardcover) / ISBN 978-0-545-48447-3 (paperback)

12 11 10 9 8 7 6 5 4 3 2 1   13 14 15 16 17 18/0

Printed in China   38
First Scholastic printing, June 2013

Meet Boris.
He's a lot like you.

favorite book
(this week)

KOMODO
KAPERS

favorite
skateboard

favorite
pencil
case

favorite
sketch pad

favorite
duck

favorite
cat

BORIS

He lives with his mom and dad.

This is Dad.

This is Mom.

He lives in an old bus.

Boris likes to go places with his friends.

This is Alice.

This is Frederick.

And he likes to dream.

Boris dreams of big beasts.

He dreams of big shows.

And big trips.

But mostly he dreams
about big adventures!

You'll never be bored when Boris is around!
So hitch a ride for his next adventure.

He could take you anywhere . . .
the African jungle,
the wild sea, or maybe
just around the corner.

CHAPTER ONE

Boris liked pets.

He had lots of pets.

There was Lion the cat.

There were his chickens,
Ethel and Tina.

There was Frank the sheep.
And there was Quince the duck.

This week he also had six worms,

two spiders,

a large beetle,

and a tiny skink.

But what Boris really wanted
was a Komodo dragon.

What a great pet!

14

Every Tuesday he gave a talk to his class about Komodo dragons.

17

That's right, Indonesia—
a long, long way from Hogg Bay.

CHAPTER TWO

Mom and Dad and Boris
were having dinner.

Then Dad had an idea.

What about the zoo?

We could visit their Komodo dragon.

This gave
Boris an even
better idea.

That night he wrote a letter.

To: The Keeper
At: the Zoo
Dear Zoo Keeper,
Would your Komodo
dragon
like a Vacation?
He could come to our
house. It's at 24 Sprig
Rd, Hogg Bay. Come
at 9 o'clock on
Saturday morning.
We live in a van.
Your friend,
Boris

Boris found
an envelope.

He found a stamp.

And he mailed the letter.

CHAPTER THREE

The next morning, Boris couldn't
wait to get to school.

He couldn't wait to tell his friends,
Frederick and Alice.

Komodo dragons bothered
Frederick, with their sharp teeth
and poisonous spit.

Over the next few days, they built
a house for the Komodo dragon.

Alice and Boris made a poster.
Ms. Constance the librarian helped
them make copies.

Soon the whole school was
talking about Boris and his
Komodo dragon.

CHAPTER FOUR

Finally it was Friday afternoon.
Only one more sleep to go.

Dr. Clara Price
City Zoo
Safari St.
Hogg City

Dear Boris,
Thank you so much for your letter. Unfortunately, our Komodo dragon does not take vacations. Perhaps you'd like to visit it instead. We'd love to see you!
Best wishes,

Dr. Clara Price
Head Keeper
Department of Reptiles

Boris needed to think.

That night he thought very hard.

CHAPTER FIVE

He was still thinking
the next morning.

Boris took a deep breath
and went outside.

And there in the cage, sitting on
a rock in the sun, was a tiny lizard.

The lizard was very still.

Until . . .

For a moment, no one said
anything. Then . . .

There was panic.

Everyone ran for their lives.

Well, nearly everyone.

Now there was no Komodo
dragon and no skink.

CHAPTER SIX

Boris said good-bye
to Frederick and Alice.

He walked back
to his room.

He had another look at the letter.

And that's
when he
finally saw ...

... what else
was in the
envelope.

That afternoon, the whole family
went to the zoo. Frederick and
Alice came as well.

Alice fed the seals.

Frederick held
a snake.

And Boris got to see
a real Komodo dragon.

It was very big. And a bit sleepy.

They met Dr. Price. She knew
a lot about Komodo dragons.

Even more than Boris.

Young Komodo dragons live in trees until the age of four.

That night Boris looked
at his photos from the zoo.

He still liked Komodo dragons.

But he thought
that next Tuesday . . .

... he might talk
about something else.

THE END

HOW TO MAKE A LIZARD PUPPET

BY BORIS

THINGS YOU NEED:

1. An old sock—a long sock works best

2. Googly eyes or buttons

3. Red felt or a piece of scrap fabric

4. Yellow felt or another piece of scrap fabric

5. Craft glue or a needle and thread

6. Fabric paint or permanent marker

7. Other bits and pieces for decoration. Think about things like ribbons, cardboard, buttons, and beads.

Now turn the page....

STEP 1: Pull the sock down tightly over your arm and use your hand to form a mouth.

STEP 2: Take off your sock and ask an adult for help with the next steps.

STEP 3: *GET DECORATING!*
You can add:
- Some googly eyes.
  (Or you can use your buttons.)
- A circle of red felt or fabric for the mouth.
- A piece of yellow felt or fabric for the tongue.

STEP 4: *USE YOUR IMAGINATION!* Add some scaly legs and pointy spikes. Paint, draw, or sew a pattern on its body.

NOW YOU'VE MADE A LIZARD!

You'll never be bored when **BORIS** is around! Look for his next exciting adventure:

It's Field Day, and Boris is ready to run like he's never run before. He wants to beat Eddie, who always wins everything. All his friend Frederick wants is not to come in last . . . again.

Who will make it across the finish line first? And when Boris is faced with a big decision, will he go for the gold or help a friend in need? Ready, set, go!

As a boy, **ANDREW JOYNER** had lots and lots
of pet lizards. Shinglebacks, blue-tongues,
bearded dragons, even a twelve-inch-long
eastern water skink, which one day escaped
into his mom's Volvo, never to be seen again.
Maybe it's still there. But he could never
get his hands on a Komodo dragon. Just
as well, though—they don't like Volvos.